The Little Toymaker

Cat Min

LQ
LEVINE QUERIDO
Montclair | Amsterdam | Hoboken

In a faraway land, on top of a rainbow mountain, there was an old wooden tower.

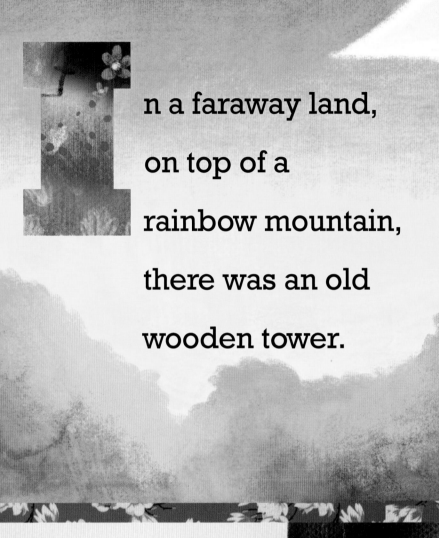

Inside, the Little Toymaker kept himself busy making toys.

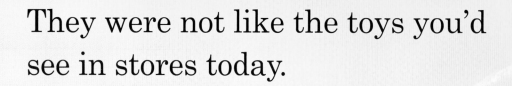

They were not like the toys you'd
see in stores today.

They were magical; each
and every one of them
was unique.

And it might surprise you that the Little Toymaker did not make these toys for himself or for children.

He made toys for grandparents, for older people. People often forgot that they, too, liked toys.

Imagine your grandmother,
making her way up to the old
wooden tower, bringing with her
a toy from her childhood.

When anyone brought an old toy, the Little Toymaker would rebuild it into something new—something magical.

Well, one day, early in the morning, there was a soft knock at the door.

"Hello. Are you the Little Toymaker?"

"Good morning!
Come in!"

"I used to play with this candy tin when I was a little girl. Once I finished all the candy, I'd fill it up with pebbles and shake it," said the old lady.

"I know exactly what to do!" said the Little Toymaker.

The Little Toymaker went to his working table. While he worked, he and the old lady began to talk.

They talked about the weather. They talked about their favorite colors.

His was indigo. Hers was coral.

They talked about what they liked and
didn't like. They both kept a garden.
He grew flowers. She grew vegetables.
He wondered if she liked flowers.
She didn't mind them.

After an hour, the Little Toymaker
returned with the candy tin.

"Here's the new
toy you've been
waiting for!"

"Ta-dah!

"Ack!"

But the old lady was crestfallen.
 "Um, no… this isn't what I'm looking for,"
said the old lady.
 "Hmmm. A-ah! I have just the thing,"
said the Little Toymaker.

"Oh dear.
No."

"Beautiful, yes… but
not quite what I had in
mind."

"No."

"It's lovely, really. But…
I guess I don't know
exactly what I wanted…"

"Why don't we have some tea and talk some more?"

"Perfect."

"Thank you."

When the Little Toymaker returned
with jasmine tea and mooncakes,
he couldn't help but stare at the old
lady's bag.

"That bag—it's amazing,"
said the Little Toymaker.
The old lady chuckled.

"This was a gift from a boy I knew when I was young," said the old lady. "He made it himself, using what he could find in his home.

It looks old and worn now, but it was the most beautiful thing I've ever received from someone."

"It's still very beautiful."

"Oh, he also gave me this scarf."

"It reminds me of the sea under a starry night."

"Yes. He knew I loved the sea," said the old lady.

"He must be special to you," said the Little Toymaker.

The old lady smiled sadly.

"Yes, he was…"

The old lady
sighed and closed
her eyes. Soon
she was asleep.

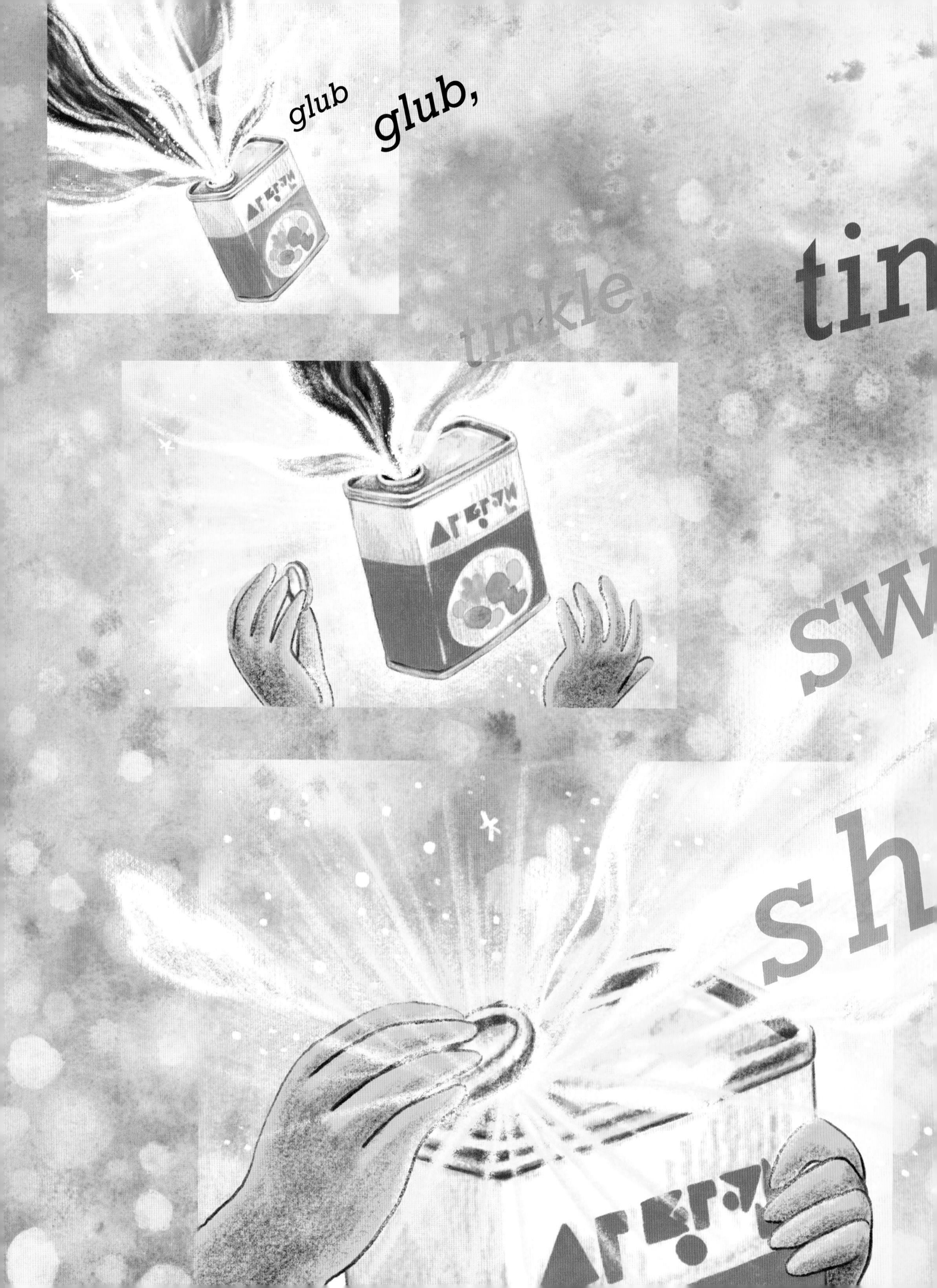
glub glub,
tinkle,
tin
sw
sh

"If you've given up on helping me, I understand. I should be heading home now…"

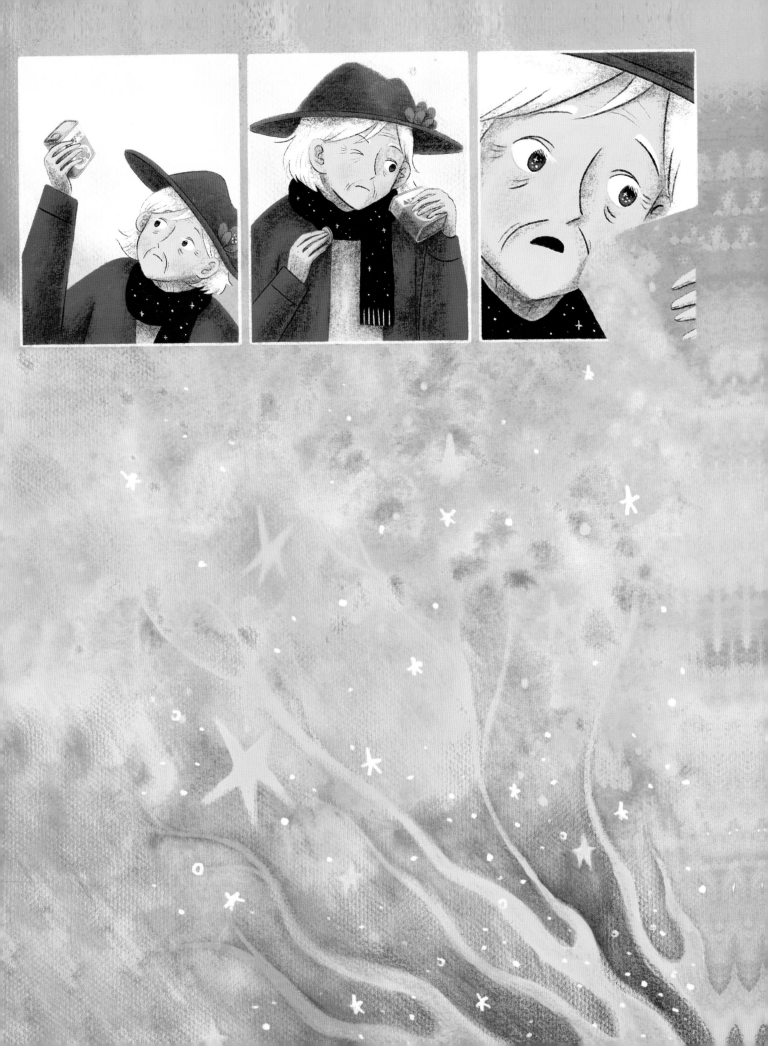

"How...
How did you
know?"

"It was your story, that *you* told me. Thank you for sharing it with me."

Beaming, the old lady left, hugging the candy tin tightly against her heart all the way home.

The Little Toymaker went back to his working table, and every once in a while he would touch the flower in his head, remembering that toys were magic. For everyone.

For KASTOR & POLLUX,
my two little toymakers

This is an Arthur A. Levine book
Published by Levine Querido

LQ
LEVINE QUERIDO

www.levinequerido.com
info@levinequerido.com

Levine Querido is
distributed by
Chronicle
Books, LLC

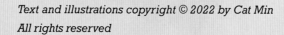

Text and illustrations copyright © 2022 by Cat Min

Library of Congress Control Number: 2022931610
ISBN 978-1-64614-180-7
Printed and bound in China

FSC
www.fsc.org

MIX
Paper from
responsible sources
FSC™ C104723

Published in October 2022
First Printing

Book design by Joy Chu
The text type was set in Century and Rockwell
The display type was set in Rockwell Extra Bold, layered with magic
dust by Cat Min